P9-DIF-238

Andy and His Yellow Frisbee

Written and Illustrated
by Mary Thompson

Woodbine House   1996

Andy was a real puzzle to Sarah. Sarah had noticed him her first day at her new school.

Andy looked like any other kid. But he sure didn't behave like any other kid. Every day at recess, Andy spun his yellow frisbee. First he picked a flat spot on the playground. Then he set his yellow frisbee on its edge. And with a flick of his fingers, he made it spin around and around and around.

Around and around went the frisbee. Around and around and around, all recess long.

Sometimes Sarah saw a girl with Andy, a girl named Rosie. Sarah figured that Rosie was Andy's sister. Except for Rosie, Andy always stayed by himself, spinning the yellow frisbee around and around and around.

What, Sarah wondered, was going on with Andy and his yellow frisbee?

Sarah zipped her backpack closed, pulled it on, and went out to the playground for recess.

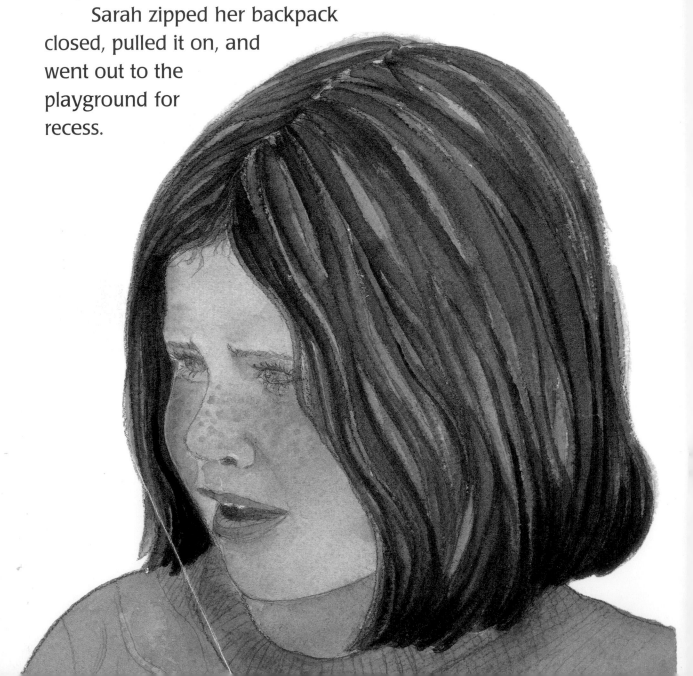

The lunch recess was the longest recess and that's when Rosie liked to play soccer. Today Rosie's game was hectic. Her team was way behind, and they were working hard to catch up. Even so, Rosie kept an eye out for her little brother, Andy. Andy was near the hopscotch, spinning the yellow frisbee that he always brought from home.

Around and around went the frisbee. Around and around and around.

Rosie was used to Andy spinning things. He spun coins so fast they were a flash of light. He could spin dinner plates without breaking them. He could spin in a tire swing faster and farther than anyone.

Andy definitely had a special talent for spinning stuff around. But, Rosie thought, understanding Andy wasn't as simple as knowing that he had a special talent. Nothing was simple about her brother. Mom had told her that was because Andy had autism.

Andy liked to keep to himself. Even when he was a baby he didn't want to be held or cuddled.

Of course, just about everyone likes a little time to themselves. But it was different for Andy. It seemed like Andy wanted to be in his own world just about all the time. And he didn't let anyone else in. He never said what he was thinking, or how he was feeling.

Even if he did want to tell, he had a tough time talking. It was as if his words were stuck somewhere inside him, and couldn't get out.

And maybe because he had such trouble with words, or maybe because he had a hard time with other people and new situations, Andy could get pretty upset. And when Andy got upset, he shut his eyes, wrapped his arms around his ears, and screamed and screamed and screamed.

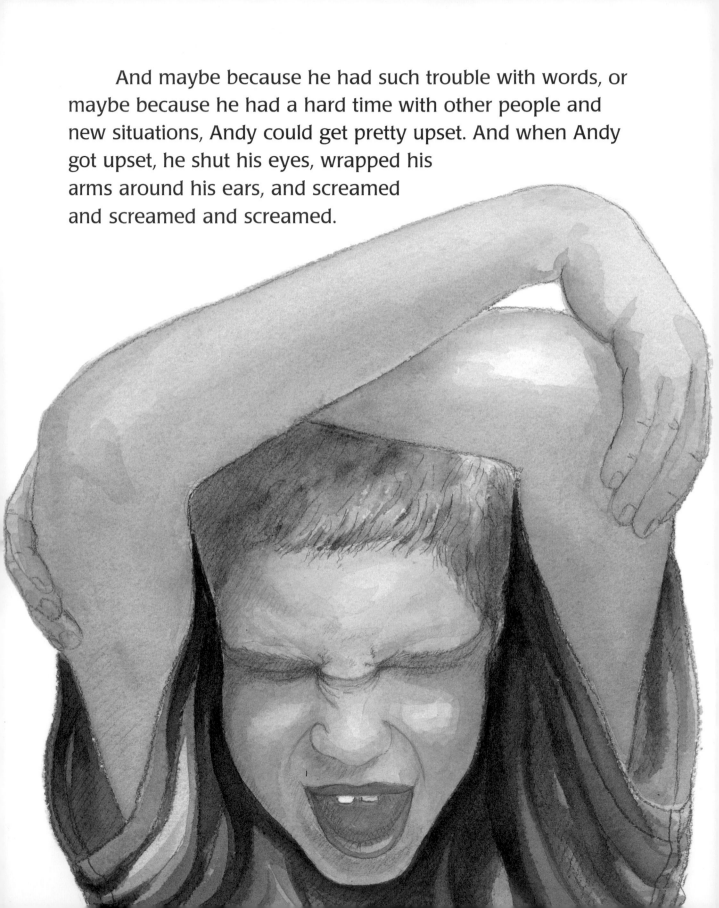

The next time Rosie looked up from her soccer game to check on Andy, she saw a girl sort of hanging around, watching him spin his yellow frisbee. It was the new girl at school, the one with the big backpack.

Rosie was worried. She thought that the new girl might not understand about Andy. And she was pretty sure that Andy didn't have the words to deal with the new girl. She knew how upset he could get. So she kicked the ball to a fast little second-grader and ran over toward Andy, just in case.

When Rosie got nearer,
she saw that the new girl
was holding a frisbee, too.
It was just like Andy's,
only pink.

"That's really cool, the
way you can spin that
frisbee," Rosie heard
Sarah say to Andy.

Andy just kept
spinning his yellow frisbee.
Around and around
went the frisbee.
Around and around
and around.

"Will you show me how you do it?" Sarah asked Andy.

Then Sarah sat down, right next to Andy. "You can try mine if you like," she said. Sarah set her pink frisbee on the ground in front of him.

Andy looked at Sarah's pink frisbee, out of the corner of his eye. His yellow frisbee wobbled, and fell over on its side with a plop.

Sarah sat still and waited. She hoped that Andy might answer her, or maybe even pick up her frisbee and start playing with it. But he didn't.

Instead, he picked up his own frisbee. He moved a little bit away, set his frisbee on its edge again, and spun it into a yellow blur.

Around and around went the frisbee. Around and around and around.

All around them, kids chased each other and yelled and tumbled and threw balls and hollered on the swings and hung on the monkey bars. It seemed to Sarah that Andy and his yellow frisbee were a little island of quiet on the busy school playground.

Sarah thought about how it was for her to be the new girl at school. Each day, finding her way around the building, meeting her teachers, making friends, was kind of scary.

Every morning Sarah packed her favorite teddy, the big brown teddy, into her backpack. Just knowing that her teddy was with her wherever she went gave Sarah the extra comfort that she needed for now.

Maybe, Sarah thought, maybe Andy's spinning yellow frisbee was something like that.

Sarah picked up her pink
frisbee and stood up. "That's OK,
Andy," Sarah said. "How about
another time?"
Sarah turned to reach
for her backpack and saw
Rosie standing there,
watching Andy spinning
his yellow frisbee.
Around and around
went the frisbee. Around
and around and around.

Rosie saw that her brother seemed to be in his own world again, spinning the frisbee around by himself. The new girl had gotten awfully close, closer than Andy usually liked, and Rosie had been afraid that he might have some trouble. But he didn't.

Instead, Andy made Rosie wonder. Rosie knew that nothing was simple about Andy. And she decided that the pink frisbee looked pretty nice. Maybe, Rosie thought, another time he *will* show the new girl how to spin a frisbee, around and around and around.

Rosie looked across the playground for her soccer game. But the game was over for today.

Sarah almost put her pink frisbee back into her back-pack with the big brown teddy. Instead, she held the pink frisbee out, to Rosie this time. "I'm Sarah," she said. "Want to play catch?"

Rosie took hold of Sarah's pink frisbee. "Sure," she said. "Let's play."

Around and around went the frisbee. Around and around and around.

What Is Autism?

Autism is a disability that affects about 400,000 children and adults in the United States. No one knows for sure what causes it. But we do know that autism is not catching, like chicken pox. Autism usually appears before a child is age three.

Like Andy, many children with autism are not sure how to deal with other people, even though they may really want to have friends. They may not want to be touched or may have difficulty looking at or listening to others. In addition, children with autism often have difficulty talking and trouble understanding what other people say.

Children with autism may seem to be more interested in toys than people. Instead of playing imaginatively, they may repeat the same action over and over. They may keep lining up toy cars, stacking blocks, or spinning toys and objects like Andy does.

Many children with autism feel sensory input (sounds, sights, smells, tastes, and touches) differently than other children do. For example, ordinary sounds may feel very loud, even painful, to their ears. Perhaps spinning a frisbee around and around, or other repetitive play like this, helps them deal with sensations. It may help them to organize a jumble of confusing sensations and to feel more in control of their world.

No two children with autism are exactly alike. But they are all more like other children than different from them. With extra care and support at home and at school, they can learn important skills and become a valuable part of their community.